In Memoriam

Brother
HUEY P. NEWTON

Sister
LOUISE DUNLAP

Dedication:

Bro. Haki Madhubuti
Bro. Gil-Scott Heron
Bro. Maulana Karenga
Bro. Segun Shabaka
Bro. Molefi Asante
Bro. Jitu Weusi
Bro. Etherero Akinshegun
who continue to shape our world . . .

And to others, sisters and brothers, who dare to define and defend our images and our interests.

AESOP: TALES OF AETHIOP THE AFRICAN, VOL. I

Flying Lion Press
A division of Sea Island Information Group

ISBN: 1-877610-03-8

Ilustrations by Demba Mbengue
c Copyright, 1989, Jamal Koram

Cover Design by the Author
Cover Re-illustrated by Marci Dunn Ramsey

AESOP: TALES OF AETHIOP THE AFRICAN, VOL. I is available on audio cassette tape

Manufactured in the United States of America

Flying Lion Press
Sea Island Information Group
P.O. Box 10628
Silver Spring, Maryland 20904
301-937-2494

TABLE OF CONTENTS

Illustrations

INTRODUCTION

Aethiop, or Aesop, lived during the sixth century B.C. He is said to have come from Cotieum, Phrygia, Asia Minor. He was a Black man. For a while he lived on the isle of Samos, in Greece, and later moved to Athens. He lived in Athens for some time.

During his youth, Aethiop was a shepherd boy. He grew to be one of the most prominent and famous people of that time and place. He was an orator and a counsellor. He was a statesman and a philosopher, and a student of the African "mystery schools." Aethiop was an honored guest at the courts of emperors and kings. It is said that every ancient Greek author either quoted or mentioned Aethiop in their writings. Lysippus, the sculptor, erected a statue in his memory. As a testimony to his greatness, his fables have been handed down for more than two thousand years.

The moral, and political wisdom of his fables are found in all parts of the English language. Such phrases as "Be prepared," "Sour Grapes," "Don't count your chickens before they hatch," and one good turn deserves another," are integral parts of ordinary speech and folklore.

Indeed, many authors have added their own signatures, and additions to the fables; and I add my versions to the list. In this first of three volumes of "Aesop," the tone of the following volumes are sure to come out. In these volumes, Aesop is decidedly African--his Greek address notwithstanding. The stories will contain elements of the Swahili, the Wolof, the Zulu, the Gullah and other African Americans; and will use tidbits of language from Africa and the African diaspora.

In these stories, you will read of the Civet, the Shoebill Stork, and the Ikiti. You will learn the names of trees like the Baobab, the Acacia, the Pine, and the Oak-- all in the same forest!

Of course, some liberties have been taken, with names of nations, and with personal names, but we have attempted to stay as close to reality as possible. These collections of stories, along with the truisms, proverbs, and morals, will hopefully delight you and your family for a long time to come.

The illustrations by Demba Mbengue highlight the stories so well that the authenticity of the origins of the stories leave little room for doubt. Enjoy, Enjoy, Enjoy! Teach, Teach, Teach!

Peace and Blessings,
Jamal Koram the StoryMan

Preface

Africa! A wonderous continent with a history that spans millions of years, and hundreds of civilizations. It is the place where the history of the modern era began. Africa has given birth to science, math, medicine, dentistry, industry, architecture, the concept of one god, and the importance of the family to a nation.

In modern times it has become the home to many species of colorful, dangerous, and exotic animals. Some of these life forms have become extinct, others are on the verge of extinction, and still others continue to live in abundant numbers.

Many of us, in the western hemisphere, do not know of the variety of animals in Africa. We are even more ignorant of the peoples who have lived on this continent for millions of years. Part of the intent in writing these volumes is to educate the reader, through an Africanized account of the people, languages, and wildlife that Aesop, the African, could have used as he defended his clients with stories, parables, and riddles so indicative of the African mystery schools which he probably attended.

The stories in Volume One are value and moral laden and speak to the need to be principled; to be courageous; and to be oneself. These stories are written to be enjoyed by all, but, definitively, speak through the history and experiences of African Americans and should be understood by us. Indeed, we can learn from the experiences of others, however, the lessons must be applied for the benefit of self, family, and Nation. I welcome you to the lands of the Serengeti, to Senegal, and to the swift Sassaby. You will hear from old time favorites like the fox, the rabbit, and the porcupine, but most importantly, through my interpretations, you will be exposed to the wisdom of the African sage called Aesop, or Aethiop by the Greek people. Please listen to the lessons.

Please read to those who cannot. Please read to the children and help them to understand the messages. Above all, enjoy.

Jamal Koram the StoryMan
Dakar, Senegal

The Stories and Their Lessons

16. THE SCHOLAR AND THE LION
   "Self preservation is the first law of nature."
17. THE CROW OF KEUR SAMB
   "Where force fails, patience and endurance will often succeed."
18. THE ZEBRA AND THE SASSABY
   "...freedom is too high a price to pay for payback."
19. THE SENALGALESE FISHERMAN
   "Today is tomorrow yesterday. Live for today, plan for tomorrow, remember yesterday."
20. QUEEN LIONESS
   "Let us raise our children like the Queens and Kings they are."
21. THE DIALLI IS CAPTURED
   "Courage allows us to be creative. Use your creativity for the benefit of the people. Always challenge the enemy with your art.
22. THE GREEDY MAN AND THE GOLDEN EGGS
   "It is a greedy person that does not learn that enough is enough."
23. THE BOY WHO CRIED WOLF
   "Don't call for help if you don't need it."
24. TALK TO THE WOOD
   "Never betray the community--Never betray the unity."
25. THE HYENA AND THE BABY SUNI ANTELOPE
   "Evil needs no excuse to act."
26. THE JACKAL AND THE POTTO
   "In critical times, your wits should get sharper."
27. THE LEMUR, THE HYENA, AND THE LION
   "Traitors and cowards can never be trusted."
   "Betrayal is its own reward."
28. THE FLIES IN THE HONEY
   "Never follow a crowd. Always depend on your thoughts and intuition."
29. THE ETHIOPIAN CAPTIVE IN THE GOTH TRIBE
   "Your are only a slave if you accept your captivity. Always seek freedom."

ABOUT THE AUTHOR

M. Chionesu-Jamal R. Koram is Jamal Koram the StoryMan. He is a master storyteller from Baltimore, Maryland. His Afrocentric approach to storytelling distinguishes him among contemporary tellers, and enables him to pass on the values and culture that is inherently Afrikan-American, and is traditionally African.

Mr. Koram has performed for the International Association of Black Storytellers Festivals, the National Gullah Festival, Colonial Crafts Weekend of Virginia, Maryland's Celebration Africa, and other festivals and storytelling events. He has appeared on public radio in Houston, Baltimore, and New York, and has been seen on the NBC and BET television networks.

His stories span the African diaspora, and include Anansi Tales, Br'er Rabbit Tales, Lion Tales, and stories related to contemporary events and personalities. His songs are delightful, as is his drumming. Mr. Koram holds a B.A. degree from SUNY New Paltz, a M.S. degree from SUNY Albany, and an Ed.S degree from the University of Virginia. He is educational consultant, and conducts training workshops on a variety of youth related topics.

Mr. Koram is the author of *When Lions Could Fly; Aesop: Tales of Aethiop the African, Volume I;* and *Gifts of the Elders.* He has also edited *An Artistic Treasury of African American Giants.*

ABOUT THE ARTIST

Demba Mbengue is noted for his creative genius as lead Artist for the world famous DeCasa African Cultural and Heritage Center in Dakar, Senegal. At DeCasa he has produced the artwork for their prized sandpaintings. Mr. Mbengue has demonstrated his skill for more than 20 years, and his murals and other works can be seen in national governmental buildings throughout Dakar. He is a commissioned artist whose illustrations were most welcome for this publication.

The Author and Artist can be reached through:

SEA ISLAND INFORMATION GROUP
P.O. Box 10628
Silver Spring, MD 20904
301-937-2494

THE PORCUPINE AND THE MOLES
As told by Jamal Koram the StoryMan

*"Never open the doors of your home to your enemies.
Never give the enemy access to your generations."*

In a cold area of east Africa a porcupine could not find food nor
shelter. Other Porcupines were dying of disease and hunger.
This porcupine heard of a warmer climate in a land to the south,
and left his home. He came to a warm place where there lived
a community of Moles. "Please," said the Porcupine, "I am
hungry and ill. Please let me share your home until I get better."

Now, the Moles lived in a very small house, but being good
African people, they told the visitor that it was o.k. to stay for a
few days. However, every time the Moles would move around in
their house they would get pierced by the sharp quills of the
Porcupine. This went on for many, many days. The Moles took
this for as long as they could and finally they asked their guest to
leave.

"I don't think so," said the rude Porcupine. "I like it here. If you
are unhappy, you can leave," he exclaimed! This enraged the
Moles, who were no match for the sharp quills of the Porcupine.
So one night, they poisoned his food, and were rid of their
unwanted guest. Too late did the African Moles learn that:

*before you open the doors of your house to some one,
know who they are, where they come from, and what
their intentions are.*

THE FOX AND THE GOAT
As told by Jamal Koram the StoryMan

"Every smiling face don't mean you no good."

"Hey, Br'er [Fox]," shouted the Goat, "what you doing down in that well?" "Getting some water, my good friend. You know, this water is great!" What the fox did not say, was that he fell in the well and couldn't get out. "Friend Goat," the cunning fox shouted, "you have never tasted better water in all your life. I'll save some for you."

"Oh no you don't, don't save me nothing," exclaimed the Goat, and he leaped into the well without thinking. Quick as a wink, the fox jumped on the Goat's back, up his horns, and jumped out of the well. It was then that Goat realized he had been tricked. "Say, Brother Fox, help me out of here," cried the Goat!

"I'll help you this time," said the fox, "but the next time, you better use your head and look before you leap."

THE BOY WHO CRIED WOLF
By Jamal Koram the StoryMan
For Dr. Hugh Morgan - BROTHER BLUE

To be sung.

"Don't call for help if you don't need it."

There was a little boy.
Watched over the sheep.

He watched them everyday.
No time to play.

One day the boy he got lonely
The boy he cried, "WOLFA! WOLFA!"
He cried, "WOLFA! WOLFA!"

And the people in town, they heard this sound, they said, "that boy's in trouble up there.
So they dropped all their things and they came a running, and the boy said, "Whooowee, ha, ha, ha, ha! THERE AIN'T NO WOLF UP HERE!"

Same little boy.
Watching over the sheep.

He watched them everyday.
No time to play.

One day the boy he got lonely
The boy he cried, "WOLFA! WOLFA!"
He cried, "WOLFA! WOLFA!"

And the people in town they heard this sound they said "that boy's in trouble up there!"
So they dropped all their things, and they came a running, and the boy said, "Whoowee, ha, ha, ha, ha! THERE AIN'T NO WOLF UP HERE!"

Now, this same little boy.
Watched over the sheep.

He watched them everyday.
No time to play.

One day the Wolf he came walking
The Wolf he say, "I'm the WOLFA!"
He say, "I'M THE WOLFA!"

And the boy cried, "WOLFA! WOLFA!"
"WOLFA! WOLFA!"

And the people in town, they heard this sound, they say, 'There ain't no wolf up there." So they kept all their things, and they kept a working, and boy say, "BUT, THERE'S REALLY A WOLF UP HERE!"

He cried,
"WOLFA! WOLFA!'
And the Wolf kept getting closer.

"WOLFA! WOLFA!'
And the Wolf was real close.

"WOLFA! WOLFA!"
And the Wolfa was almost on him.!

"WOLFA!! WOLFA!!"
He could feel the Wolf's breath!

"WOLFA. WOLP . . .!

And that was the end of the boy who cried wolf.

> *Never tell lies.*
> *Never call for help when you don't need it.*
> *Be creative in your work, and you won't get tired.*
> *Be cheerful in your work and you won't be lonely.*

THE HIDDEN TREASURE
By Jamal Koram the StoryMan

"Hard work towards a worthwhile goal brings great wealth."

An old farmer, near Rufisque, was dying and he called his four children to him. As he lay close to death, he said that he would die happy if he knew that his children would continue to work and make the mango orchards prosper. He called his children to him and told them softly, but firmly, "There is hidden, in the soil, a great treasure." Soon afterwards, the farmer passed on. No sooner had their father been buried, then the children began to hunt for the treasure.

With hoes and shovels and plows, they turned the soil over, underneath each mango tree. Acre after acre, they searched for the treasure, but they found neither silver, nor gold, nor precious stones. As they turned the soil, however, the roots of the trees grew stronger, and the trees grew larger and began to yield more of this tasty and juicy fruit. One evening, while looking over the orchards, the children realized what their father had done.

"You know," said the eldest daughter, "I know now of the treasure that our father spoke of. The treasure is the orchards which are now worth more than ever." The others agreed, for they had learned a great lesson.

The StoryMan says: I have hidden a great treasure in your science, and math books; and in your history and language books.

Search for this treasure. Search for it. Search for it.

THE ELDER AND THE DOCTOR
Adapted by Jamal Koram the StoryMan

"To know yourself is to heal yourself."

An elder woke up one morning and had lost the sight in her eyes. She called a physician. She said," Doctor, if you cure me of this blindness, I will reward you well. If I remain blind, however, I will pay you nothing." "Is that a deal," she asked? The shifty eyed physician agreed.

Once a week he came to her and put some petroleum jelley on her eyes. Each time, he would also steal a piece of furniture, or some other goods. Every week this continued until almost all of her possessions were gone. Then the healer gave her a herbal remedy that cured her and restored her sight. When her vision cleared, she saw that her house was almost empty, and she refused to pay the physician.

"You better pay up," he shouted, "Or I'm taking you to the court of elders!" "Take me to court then, you thieving rascal," yelled the woman.

In the courtyard of the elders, the physician told of the agreement with the woman, and that she refused to pay him. The woman agreed. "He speaks the truth," she said. "I did agree to pay him if I got my sight back, and he agreed that he would get nothing if my sight wasn't restored." "Wise elders," she continued, "I must still be blind, for when I lost my vision, I had a house full of furniture, yet now I can't see any of it. It is all gone!"

The elders listened, and they ruled in favor of the old woman. Why?

Because those who take what is not theirs must be ready to lose what is theirs.

Treachery and treason is rewarded by tremendous loss-- Now, or later. In this generation or in future ones.

THE DONKEY AND THE MONKEY
Adapted by Jamal Koram the StoryMan

"You can't always do what you see everyone else do."

A monkey was on the roof. He was dancing and jumping around, making funny sounds. The owner of the house laughed and laughed at the monkey's antics. That afternoon, the donkey, who had watched the monkey, climbed up on the roof, and he commenced dancing and shouting "Hee Haw," "Hee Haw!" While he was jumping, he made a big hole in the roof. The owner climbed up on the roof and whipped the donkey. "Get off of here," he shouted!

"Why are you hitting me when you didn't hit the monkey," whined the donkey, "You laughed at him." "You, my friend," said the owner, "are not a monkey."

What is good for one, is not necessarily good for another.

THE LION AND THE WATER BUFFALOES
Adapted by Jamal Koram the StoryMan

"Respect our Unity--or die"

Old Sis Lion wanted some Buffalo meat and she was powerfully hungry. She saw some Buffalo in a field and started circling them, looking for a chance to attack one of the Buffalo.
In the field, one of the lead Buffalo saw her and said to one of the others, "Don't look now, but Sis Lion is trying to sneak up on us."

"What," said the other Buffalo, looking around!   "Where, where?"

"I told you don't look, dummy. Listen, tell the others to form a circle, back-to-back." Just at that moment, the Lion decided to attack. By the time she reached the Buffalo, they had formed the circle. All Sis Lion could do was pace around and around, or get a face full of horns.

Each day the Lion tried to get the Buffalo, and each day they formed a circle and held her off. One day, the lead Buffalo said, "I'm glad I thought of a way to keep the Lion off of us."
"What do you mean YOU thought of it," said another. "Don't you mean WE."

"No, I mean just what I said, knucklehead. I thought of it."
"Hold on now, who you calling names," said the second Buffalo?

"You and your Mama," said the first Buffalo!
"Least my Mama ain't jump over no moon," responded the second Buffalo.

They argued back and forth, and soon began fighting. Meanwhile, the Lion was just waiting and watching. It wasn't long before all of the Buffalo were arguing, and soon none of them were speaking to one another. Each of them went to different parts of the field to eat. Sis Lion waited no longer. One by one, she attacked the Buffalo and ate them.

United we stand, divided we fall.
Respect our mothers.
Don't let anyone or anything destroy our unity or our love for the motherland.

THE DIALLI IS CAPTURED
Adapted by Jamal Koram the StoryMan

"Courage allows us to be Creative"

When warriors would march into battle, the Dialli would motivate them, and rally them onward with his songs of valor. Playing on the xalam, he would sing of past battles and deeds of bravery.

One day, during a fierce battle, the Dialli was captured and taken prisoner. He cried out, "Don't kill me please, I haven't killed any of your people!" "See, he exclaimed, "I don't have any weapons, all I carry is this xalam." The warrior in charge said, "And that instrument is why you will die." "Indeed, you do not fight yourself, he said, "but your songs makes your soldiers fight hard.

Use your creativity for the benefit of the people.
Always challenge the enemy with your art.

He who shares in a battle with words and deeds is as
brave as he who fights.

THE ZEBRA AND THE IKITI
Adapted by Jamal Koram the StoryMan

"...freedom is to high a price to pay for payback."

A Zebra lived by himself on the Serengeti Plains. One day an Ikiti came and asked the Zebra if he could share the eating lands. "Of course you may," said the Zebra, "but only for a few days."

Ikiti stayed longer than a few days, and didn't leave when the Zebra reminded him of their agreement. This angered the striped animal, and he plotted against the Ikiti.

One day a Kikuyu hunter came hunting for a riding animal, and the Zebra asked if he would catch and kill the Ikiti. "The Ikiti is very, very, very fast", said the Kikuyu,"and I need your help to catch it." He said, "You must let me attach this rope to you, to guide you. And let me throw these skins on your back, so that I may ride you, while we chase the enemy."

"O.K.," said the Zebra, and the Kikuyu hunter put the rope in the Zebra's mouth and the skins on his back. Soon they chased the Ikiti away from the plains. "Asante sana," said the Zebra to the hunter. I'm glad that is done. Now you can take these skins and rope off of me."

"Ho," laughed the hunter. "Indeed, you would like me to do that, but now you must serve me. You gave up your freedom when you sought revenge. And now you know that freedom is to high a price to pay for payback!"

Never rely on your enemies for help against your own kind, for there is no help like that.

THE TERRAPIN AND THE HARE
Adapted by Jamal Koram the StoryMan

"Thinking, Seeing, and Hearing travel faster than Walking."

You know the hare is a very quick animal, always darting here and there.   Last Wednesday, he was bragging and wolfing at everyone about how fast he was.   "Ain't but three fast animals in the world," he boasted, "me, myself, and I."   "And I is the fastest of the three," he laughed.

Then he started signifying.   "I raced against time, and beat seconds to a minute.   I ran around the square so fast that I caught my shadow."   "I ran across the pond and didn't get wet," he said, "and I raced your fat cousin to the candy shop and beat him by a half-a-second."   "Who wants to taste some of this dust?" "Who wants a footprint san-wich?" "Huh?"

No one said a thing. The hare started again. "Chumps, huh?" "Little sissies, huh?"   "Look at you.   Who's gonna race me?"

"I'll race you, homeboy."   It was the terrapin.   The slowest thing this side of cold molasses.   "Be serious," said the hare, I'm not gonna waste my time with you." "Give me a cheetah, or a caracal, or somebody like that to race."   The terrapin said, "What's the matter, 'fraid I might beat ya?"   It took the hare about five minutes to stop laughing.   "Alright, lardbucket," he said.   "Let's boogey."

They decided to race through the woods to the pond, around Robin's barn, and back up to the square. The fox hollered, "GO!" And the race began.   The hare jumped out way in front of the Terrapin. He was moving fast as a woodpecker's head.   He got all the way to the pond, and decided to take a rest. Meanwhile, the terrapin was easing along slowly, but surely.

The hare had found some soft moss and grass to rest on. There was a nice warm breeze blowing, and he soon fell asleep.
By the time the terrapin got to the pond, the hare was in a deep sleep. His stomach was rising up and down, and he was snoring. Old terrapin kept right on past him.

Well bye and bye, the terrapin went around the barn, and was getting ready to cross the finish line when the hare woke up.
He could see the terrapin getting ready to cross the finish line, and he took off like a Bantu blow dart. It was too much, too late. The terrapin had won the race. Feeling silly, the hare hung his head and went on home.

Slow and steady wins the race, if you are racing against arrogance and stupidity. Otherwise, quick, fast, and steady wins the race against all comers.

THE SENALGALESE FISHERMAN
Adapted by Jamal Koram the StoryMan

"Today is tomorrow yesterday."
"Live for today, Plan for tomorrow, Remember Yesterday."

In N'Gor, Senegal, a fisherman had been to sea for a long while and had only caught one fish. It was a small fish, not a big fish like the Nao Nao, or Har. The fish jumped about in the Gal, or fishing boat and asked the fisherman to spare his life.

"Please Mustafa," begged the small fish, "put me back into the water. I shall become a great fish one day, large enough for many cooking fires. Then you can catch me, and that will be good profit for you."

"Dadet," said the fisherman. "No way."

"Today is today, tomorrow is tomorrow, and tomorrow is never promised."

"I will keep the catch that I have today," promised Mustafa.

A small fish in the boat is better
than a large one in the ocean.

THE CROW AND THE CIVET
Adapted by Jamal Koram the StoryMan

"Never trust those who give you false praise."

A raven feathered crow had taken a piece of cheese and was sitting on a branch about to devour it. Br'er Civet saw her with the cheese and decided that he wanted some of it.

"My, my Sis Crow," said the Civet sweetly, "You looking mighty fine sitten' up in that tree." "I was just thinking that you must be the queen of all the birds, good as you looken'."

The Crow didn' t pay any attention at first, but now she was listening. After all, the Civet was pretty good looking.

"Yes indeed, said the Civet, "Look how glossy and shiny those feathers are." "Why Sis, I mean Queen Crow, as good as you look, I bet you could sing even better."

Now Sis Crow, who was good looking, believed everything the Civet was saying to her. Without thinking, she opened her mouth to sing, and that big piece of cheese fell right into the Civet's greedy, cunning jaws. Licking his chops, the Civet said to the Crow, "Let me give you some advice: Do not ever be fooled by flattery."

> *Know yourself and love yourself, and you will always be able to separate the message from the messenger.*

TALK TO THE WOOD
Adapted by Jamal Koram the StoryMan

"It was a cold, frosty morning
the brother's mighty good
Put your axe upon your shoulder Brother
TALK to dey wood . . ."
(children's song)

There was a brother who went to the forest looking for wood to make an axe handle for his axe. The brother asked the trees to help him find the wood. An old Gimba tree said, "La, get your own wood. Don't be coming 'round here trying to start no mess."

A huge Baobab said, "Boy, if you don't get outta here, gonna be some head whipping."

"What you doing asking a tree to help you kill a tree," asked an Oak tree? "Get away from here!"

Some pines and evergreens just bowed their branches and prayed that the brother would leave. Eucalyptus trees tried to cast some aromas at him to make him go. Some maples, poplars, and birches, however, thought they could save themselves from being chopped down, so they told the brother where a young sapling was. The woodsman pulled that sapling out of the ground and made himself a strong axe handle. As soon as he fitted the axe onto the handle, he started "talking to the wood." Trees fell down all day long. The poplars and birches and maples started crying, "If only we hadn't given up that young, baby tree, maybe all of us would still be alive."

Protect your young as if
your LIFE depended on it,
and never betray the community--
never betray the unity.

THE LITTLE GREEDY BOY
Adapted by Jamal Koram the StoryMan

"Measured actions bring about solid success"

A young brother was very hungry, and so he went to a gourd that was full of delicious cashews and peanuts. He reached into the gourd and grabbed a fistfull of nuts. When he tried to pull his hand from the neck of the gourd, he could't because his hand was crammed full of nuts.

The boy did not want to give up any of the cashews and peanuts, but he also could not pull his hand free of the gourd.
He began crying BIG tears. A grandmother saw him crying, and said, "Boy, if you turn loose some of those nuts, you will be able to free your hand!"

Too much of anything will trap you.
Sometimes it is better to have half than none at all.

THE SWIMMER AND THE MZEE
Adapted by Jamal Koram the StoryMan

"Save me now. Preach to me later."

There was a young boy who loved to swim. On a hot summer day, after the soltice, he jumped into a cool inland lake at the quarry. The lake was deeper than the boy thought, and he began to thrash around, and call for help. An elder happened to be passing the quarry and saw the boy flopping around like a wounded fish.

"Young man," called the Mzee, "Don't you know better than to swim in water that is too deep for you?" "Look at you!" "What would your parents say if they saw you swimming in this lake."
"I don't know what the young folks are coming to these days."

"Mzee, Mzee," called the drowning boy, "Please save me now and preach to me later!"

In critical times, action is needed more than words.

THE GREEDY MAN AND THE GOLDEN EGGS
Adapted by Jamal Koram the StoryMan

*"It is a greedy person who does not learn
that enough is enough."*

One day in early spring, a man who had bought a goose in a foreign market, discovered that it had laid an egg of pure gold. He ran to his wife shouting, "Our goose just laid a golden egg!" The wife was very happy, and took it to the market place. She received a great amount of money for it.

The following day the goose laid another golden egg. Each day, the farmer discovered another egg, and each day the wife would take it to market in exchange for money. Soon the couple was very rich. But the husband was not satisfied. The more money he received, the more he required. Evil filled his head.

"Why," he thought, must I be content with just one egg a day? If I cut the goose open, I can get all the gold at once!" This crazy man ran out to the yard, grabbed an axe, caught the goose, who looked at him with shock and pain, and killed it. What did the greedy man find? There was no gold inside.

Those who are greedy, many times, lose everything.

QUEEN LIONESS
Adapted by Jamal Koram the StoryMan

*"Let us raise our children like the
Queens and Kings they are"*

All the animals in the forest were arguing about who gave birth to the most children. The gnu and the topi, the cheetah and the elephant, and may others were claiming the most children.

"I have five children at one time," claimed one. "So," said another, "I give birth twice a year." As everyone was talking, the Lioness walked by with her cub. "Oh, look," said the giraffe, "There's Ms. Lioness." "And how many young ones do you give birth to," she asked?"

"At first, Queen Lioness walked past the other animals, but then she turned, and with a slight smile, said, "Just one, but that one is a LION!"

Quality is better than Quantity.

THE LION AND THE FOX
Adapted by Jamal Koram the StoryMan

"It is wise to learn from other's mistakes."

The lion was getting old and feeble. His legs were stiff and his eyesight was poor. He could no longer hunt for his food. Since he could not hunt for his food, the lion knew he would soon die. And so, the old cat came up with a plan. "What I will do," he thought, "is invite my friends to my house. When they come in, I will eat them up!" This plan was good for the lion, but not so good for his friends.

One sunny day, Mister antelope came by the lion's cave. The lion called to him, "Oh, Mr. Antelope! Mr. Antelope, please come and visit me." The antelope agreed, and asked the lion how he was feeling. "My back hurts," complained the lion, "my knees hurt, and my head hurts. Please come in and fix me some tea." The Antelope said "O.K."

As he was preparing the tea, the lion crept up on him. Before the Antelope realized what was happening, the old lion had jumped on him and ate him up.

Two days later, Br'er Lion heard his friend the monkey up in the trees. "Mr. Monkey! Mr. Monkey, please come down and visit me." "O.K., said the monkey, "Howya feeling?" "Oh Mr. Monkey," said the lion, "I'm not feeling to well. My back hurts, my knees hurt, and my head hurts. Please come in and read the daily newspaper to me." "O.K.," said the monkey.

As the monkey was reading the newspaper, the Lion crept up on him. Before the monkey knew what was happening, the Lion jumped up on him and ate him up.

This unfair practice went on for days and days. Bye and bye, the fox came walking past the Lion's cave. Br'er Lion called out to him. "Mr. Fox! Mr. Fox, please come and visit me. I'm not feeling to well. I need you to come in and fix my bath water!"

Now, the Fox was a very wise and cautious animal. Around the Lion's cave, he saw many, many, many tracks and footprints going into the Lion's house, but he didn't see any footprints coming out.

"Excuse me, Brother Lion," said the Fox, knowingly,   "I see where you had a lot of visitors lately."

"Oh yes, yes," stammered the Lion, "My friends love to come and visit me."

"Well," said the Fox, I've noticed that a lot of your friends have been going into your house, but not coming out." "When those friends come out, he said, "I'll go in and fix your bath water." After saying that, the Fox trotted away, leaving the hungry Lion looking dumbfounded.

Sometimes you can use the experiences of others
to learn valuable lessons.

THE DONKEY IN THE LION'S SKIN
As told by Jamal Koram the StoryMan

*"If you don't know who you are,
you will try to be some of everybody"*

One day a Donkey found a Lion's skin, complete with head, tails, and claws. He put it over him and went into town to scare people. As soon as the townspeople saw him, they ran in fear, because they thought that the donkey was really a Lion. For a while he ran around scaring folks pretending to be a Lion.

Pretty soon, he began to think that he WAS a Lion!
He saw Br'er Goat and thought, "I'll scare him with my mighty roar." The Donkey opened his mouth to roar and out came a very LOUD "HEE-HAW! HEE-HAW!"

Br'er Goat just looked. He sucked his teeth and said, "Shucks, that ain't nobody but that jive old donkey. Had me fooled 'till he opened his mouth."

*Sometimes it is better to be yourself
and to keep your mouth shut.*

UMOJA
As told by Jamal Koram the StoryMan

*"Now, more than ever, all the family
must be together."*

A mother had many sons who were always arguing and fighting with one another. She used everything she knew to stop them from fighting. She would give them work to do. They would argue about that. She would give them books to read. They would fight about that. She tried many things to help them treat eachother well.

One day she called all of her boys and said to them:

"Your father left us all two things to be very proud of.
 He left us good land and a good name. Your constant bickering with one another would have made him very sad, and I know he would not have put up with it." "You will drive me to an early grave if you don't stop." The mother then showed the sons a bundle of sticks. She said, "I'm am only going to teach this lesson once. Anyone who doesn't learn will have to leave for good."

She then asked each of them to try and break the bundle. The strongest son tried first. He couldn't break it. And each of her many sons could not break the bundle.

The Mother then separated the bundle and gave each son a stick. "Try to break the stick," she said. Each boy snapped his stick with ease. "If we remain strong as a family, with no fighting, and by working together, we will be as strong as the bundle of sticks. But, if we are not in harmony and not productive, we will be snapped apart as easily as sticks.

In unity there is strength.

THE CROW OF KEUR SAMB
As told by Jamal Koram the StoryMan

"We must have patience and endurance."

A thirsty Crow who lived in the village of Keur Samb, came upon a carved gourd which was half-filled with spring water. Unfortunately for her, the water level was low and she couldn't drink the water because she had a short beak. The Crow tried to knock the gourd over. It was too big and heavy. Near the water gourd was a pile of small stones. One by one she dropped the stones into the vessel. [jurrum, jurrum nyet etc].

With each stone dropped, the water rose higher, and higher. [jurrum jurrum jurrum]. After she dropped ninety-nine stones in the gourd, the water had risen high enough for the crow to drink.

Where force fails, patience
and endurance will often succeed.

THE HUNTER AND THE HERBSMAN
As told by Jamal Koram the StoryMan

"Before you hunt for the truth, be prepared to meet it."

Osabi was not known as a brave hunter. But, today he was not content with hunting rabbits. On this day, he was in search of the tracks of a Lion. After searching all morning, he ran into a Herbsman who was out in the bush collecting healing medicine herbs.

"Salaam, my Brother," said the small game hunter in a big voice. "Have you seen any Lion tracks around here? "Or maybe," he laughed, "You can show me where he lives!"

IshLaWo, the wise herbsman studied the hunter, and calmly replied, "I can show you." "Come with me," he said, "I will take you to the Lion's den."

"Oh, no, no, no, no," exclaimed the hunter, "You don't understand good Brother, I'm just looking for the tracks, not for the Lion!"

A leader must be brave in deed
as well as in words.
Before you hunt for the truth,
be prepared to meet it.

THE SCHOLAR AND THE LION
As told by Jamal Koram the StoryMan

"Self Preservation is the first law of nature."

An African scholar and an old Lion were walking through the great African rainforest. They were debating about who was the strongest, Man or Lion.

As they entered a clearing in the forest, they saw a huge wooden sculpture. The sculpture was of a Masai warrior conquering a Lion. "Look there," said the Scholar, see how strong that warrior is. That proves I am right, Man is strongest."

"My Brother, My Brother," said the Lion, "this does not prove a thing." "If sculptures were made by Lions," he explained, "the Lion would be conquering the Man."

"Listen, how a story ends always depends on who the story teller is."

THE OSTRICH AND THE FARMER
As told by Jamal Koram the StoryMan

"People are known by the company they keep."

In the village of Mbeya, when a farmer plants new seeds, he also places nets over the fields to catch seed-stealing Storks. One day a farmer, named Mwengi, caught quite a few Storks, and one Ostrich.

"Please, Mwengi," whispered the Ostrich, "let me go free."
"I am not a Stork, as you can see," he said, "but an Ostrich who comes from an excellent family, and a good neighborhood." The Ostrich explained that he did not even look like "those ugly Storks."

Mwengi, the farmer, did not bat an eye. He looked at the Ostrich and said, "Indeed, what you say may be true, but I caught you with these seed stealing Storks, and I know that birds of a feather flock together."

If you are not a thief, don't hang around thieves.
If you are honest, make friends with honest people.
People are known by the company they keep.

THE LION AND THE FOREST HOG
As told by Jamal Koram the StoryMan

"Beware of the Vultures, hungry ones
will attack a Leopard."

A Lion and a wild Forest Hog wanted to drink from a small watering hole at the same time. Both of them were very thirsty. "Kai mangee naa, I'm thirsty," bellowed the Lion. "Dadet, no," growled the fierce Hog, "I drink first."

They began to argue fiercely. Hair bristled up on the Lion's back. He barred his teeth. The wild Forest Hog scraped his tusks on the rocky ground. They were about to throw down, when the shadows of flying vultures passed overhead. Both the Lion and the Forest Hog looked up.

Understanding came quickly. "Look," said the Hog, "the Vultures are waiting and anxious for us to do battle so that they can eat the loser."

The Lion agreed, and said, "let us not fight, you drink first."

When a common enemy approaches,
small differences are best forgotten.

THE HYENA AND THE BABY SUNI ANTELOPE
As told by Jamal Koram the StoryMan

"Evil needs no excuse to act"

A baby Suni was taking a bath in a brook. A Hyena saw him, and decided that a Suni would be a tasty appetizer. "I should be ashamed of myself," thought the Hyena, "attacking a small helpless animal." Still, the Hyena ran up to the Suni, and shouted, "Hey, you little hopper, what are you doing messing up my drinking water!"

"Why sir," said the Suni, "I'm standing on a rock, not in the water."

"Never mind," yelled the Hyena, "I heard you were talking about my mother last year!"

"But sir," said the Suni, I was just born last year."

"Never mind," said the Hyena, "it was probably your brother, and that's why I'm going to eat you up!" And he did.

Bad people will be bad no matter what you do.

THE JACKAL AND THE POTTO
As told by Jamal Koram the StoryMan

"In critical times, your wits should get sharper."

One day a hungry Jackal decided to hunt for her food, rather than steal from the Hyenas. She spied a large Potto, and chased it in and out of the undergrowth of the forest. Finally, the Potto scampered up a tree and got away. A young Hyena had watched the chase.

"Yo, Jackal," he called out, "you slow as molasses on a cold day!"

"You ought to be shame of yo'self."

The older Jackal answered, saying, "Young-un, understand that I was chasing my dinner. He was running for his life."

Maybe one day the Potto will
start spreading those blues around.

THE LEMUR, THE HYENA, AND THE LION
As told by Jamal Koram the StoryMan

"Traitors and Cowards Can Never be Trusted."

Two unlikely friends decided to go hunting together--the blackfaced Lemur and the Hyena. Br'er Hyena went in the bush first to flush out the game.

Br'er Hyena wasn't watching where he was going and he bumped into Sis Lion.

"Oh 'scuse me, 'scuse me," said the Hyena. "I'm so sorry, I wasn't looking where I was going." The Lion looked at the Hyena and said, "No apologies necessary, I'm going eat you anyway!"

Seeing that he was in BIG trouble, the Hyena whispered to the Lion. "Pssst, you don't have to eat me. I can show you where there's a nice fat little Lemur. I'll take you there." The Lion agreed, and as soon as she killed the unsuspecting Lemur, she chased down the Hyena and killed him too.

Betrayal is its own reward

THE FLIES IN THE HONEY
As told by Jamal Koram the StoryMan

"Never Follow a Crowd. Always depend on your thoughts and Intuition."

A child accidently knocked over a small gourd full of honey outside of his home and ran. Just then a bunch of yellow-winged flies came cruising by. A sharp-eyed fly shouted out, "Wow, look at all that honey on the ground!" As if pulled by an invisible string, the heard of flies dove into the honey. O-o-o-o Wee, the honey was good to those flies! Instead of being satisfied with eating around the edges, they went deeper and deeper in the spilled honey. Some of them were so bold, that they trudged up inside the gourd! "I'm stuck," cried a fly inside the gourd, "I can't get free." Soon all the flies realized they were trapped and could not escape. One fly, who stayed on the edges, tearfully said, "How stupid of us to lose our lives for a moment's pleasure."

Too much of a good thing is dangerous

THE ETHIOPIAN CAPTIVE IN THE GOTHIC TRIBE

*"You are only a slave if you accept
your captivity. Always seek freedom."*

In a European city, an Ethiopian captive was told by a Gothic tribal priest, to carry a large religious symbol on his chest during a parade. As the captive walked in the parade, the people bowed down as he passed them. This made his head get big.

He thought they were bowing for him. He began walking to the crowds and touching people on the heads, as if blessing them.
The priest slapped him in the back of his head, and brought him back to reality. "Foolish slave, said the priest, "they are not bowing to you, but to my symbol that you are carrying.

*Carry no one's symbol, but your own.
You symbols will look like you, be for you,
and worn only by you.*

GLOSSARY AND PRONUNCIATION GUIDE

Lion - Symbol of strength and courage, pride, dignity and African royalty.

Osabi (OH sah bee) - Afrocentric male name.

Salaam (Sah LAHM) - East African/Islamic greeting meaning "Peace."

Herbsman - A traditional African healer, found whereever there are black people.

Brother - Title reserved for black males indicating an unspoken solidarity, and a feeling of family connectiveness. Black females are called Sister.

IshLaWo (Ish LA woh) - A composite Afrocentric name formed from the names of three contemporary herbalists.

Umoja (oo MOH jah) - A word meaning 'Unity" from the African language of Kiswahili.

Gil Scott-Heron - A Pan Africanist musician known for penetrating lyrics which pose serious analysis of issues and events which affect our lives.

Harmony - Concept of peaceful living with one another.

Unity - Concept of oneness, of family, of working and living together as Africans in the global nation.

Bickering - Mindless arguing over silly and trivial pursuits.

Donkey - Symbol of stubborness, and foolishness

Goat - Symbol of analysis, wisdom, and clarity

Br'er (BRAIR) - Shortened form of "Brother."

Jive - Deceitful, not to be believed, unreliable, slick

Semilak - Artificial milk. Cow's milk is for cows. Human milk is for humans. If you mess with the genetics, some future generation will have to pay for your mess.

Elder - Respected old person.

Physician - Medical doctor who often uses chemicals to supress healing as opposed to natural remedies which promote healing.

Court - Place where judgements and interpretations of man-made laws are made.   Judges and lawyers sometime play with the lives of our people in these places.

Treachery - Planned evil doings against someone. Very often against someone who trusts or believes in you.

Treason - The act of treachery. Betrayal. Crimes against African people by African people.

Rufisque (Roo feesk) - Medium sized city in Senegal (SEN nay Gaal), West Africa.

Mango - Oval shaped tropical fruit that is good, good, good and juicy, juicy, juicy!

Orchards - Place on a farm where fruit trees are.

Benefits - Things that will help you. Something that will be good for you.

Vultures - Large birds that eat dead or dying animals.

Kahee Mangee

Naa - Means "I am thirsty" in the African language of Wolof.

Dadet - Means "No" in the African language of Wolof.

Forest Hog - African animal which resembles a Wild Boar.

Enemy - Someone who does not work in your best interests and who constantly seeks to do you harm, or to raise themselves up at your expense.

Mzee (m ZAY) - A wise older person. From the African language of Kiswahili.

Solstice - A time during the year when seasons change and energy levels are high.

Antelope - The bearer of news. A four-leg fleet-footed horned animal.

Monkey - African/Asian animal used as a symbol of foolishness, trickery, signifying.
Fox - Symbol of wisdom, analysis, shrewdness.

African - People who live on the continent of Africa, or whose foreparents were Africans, ie. all black people in the Americas have foreparents from Africa. In the cases of mixed parentage, you always go with those ancestors who had the strongest genes and who had the most melanin.
Moles - Smallish animals who live in tunnels underground.
Generations-In a nation, or, in a family, births which happen every 15 to 30 years create a new generation.
Intentions - What someone is going to do.
Quills - Sharp and hard, needle like hairs on a porcupine.

Ostrich - Large African bird that can run, but it can't fly.
Mbeya (m BAY yah) - A small city in central Africa.
Mwengi (MWENG ghee) - An Afrocentric male name.

Terrapin - A turtle.
Hare - A rabbit.
Chumps - Cowards. People who are hesitant to act. Meek persons.
Boogey - Run. Let's do it! An action oriented word.
Caracal - An African animal in the cat family that is very fast.
Cheetah - An African animal in the cat family that runs 70 miles per hour.
Woodpecker - A small bird found worldwide that pecks wood with his/her beak at about zillion times per second.
Bantu - Fearless Africans who live in central and southern Africa.

Ebony - Black.
Civet - A small African animal that is in the cat family.

Scholar - Person who studies books and important works of knowledge and wisdom.

Masai (Mah SIG Hee) - Fearless Africans who live in East Africa.

Rainforest - There are no jungles in Africa, they are rainforests which are important to the health of the planet

Crow - In Senegal, there lives a Crow-like bird with a white band around his body. That is the Crow of Keur Samb. Keur *Samb*(KUR Sahmb) - Means "The House of Samb" many villages and towns in West Africa are named in this way.

Zebra - A horselike African animal which is the symbol of confusion.

Sassaby - African animal in the antelope family.

Serengeti (Sayr ren ghett tee) - An extremely large system of plains in East Africa where hundreds of species of African animals live.

Kikuyu (Kee KOO Yoo) - Fearless African people who live in East Africa.

Freedom - Being able to live without fear on land that belongs to your people.

Asante Sana (Ah SAHN tay   SAH nah) - Means "Thank you very much" in the African language of Kiswahili.

Senalgalese (Sen nah gah lees) - An industrious and fearless African people living in West Africa.

N'Gor (N GOOR) - A small fishing village in Senegal.

Mustafa (Moo STAHH fah) - A common African/Islamic name.

Gnu(Ngu: N goo) - Large African antelope with an ox-like head

Topi (TOE pee) - African antelope.

Giraffe - African animal that is the tallest four legged animal in the world.

Lioness - Female lion. Symbol of royalty, dedication, and courage. A fierce hunter.

Dialli/Jali (Jolly) - African oral historian and praise singer. Also called a Griot(GREE oh).
Xalam(HAH lum) - Stringed instrument used by the Dialli.

Brother Blue - Dr. Hugh Morgan. One of the elders of African -American Storytelling. Tells stories in a jazz-like idiom and style. Revered for the spiritual presence he brings to the storytelling environment.
Wolfa - Wolf

Dey - The.
Gimba - Type of African wood.
Evergreens - Trees like pines, hemlocks, and evergreen oaks.
Eucalyptus - Evergreen trees with aromatic oils, and resins.
Maples - Leafy trees whose sap is used for syrup.
Poplars - A quick growing tree in the willow tree family.
Birches - A short lived tree whose bark peels easily.

Hyena - An dog-like powerful African animal which feeds on dead and dying animals. Symbol of treachery and deceit.
Suni Antelope - A small African antelope.

Critical - Something that requires immediate attention.
Jackal - A dog-like African animal. Symbol of cowardice, and immoral behavior.
Potto - A small African animal in the monkey family. Symbol of quick thinking, and weakness.

Traitor - Someone who commits acts of treason.
Coward - Someone who lacks courage, who acts in a disgraceful way, and who should be avoided.
Lemur - Soft and wooly African animal related to monkeys, and has the face of a fox. Symbol of simplicity and naivete.

Gourd - A plant in the pumpkin and squash family used for drinking, carrying water, sifting grains, and for African instruments.

Ethiopian - An African from the great and ancient land of Ethiopia.

European - Someone descended from any of the tribes of Europe such as the Visigoths, Barbarians, Teutons, Romans and others.

Goth - Group of western European tribes form what is now Germany and France.

Tribe - Originally, people from one of the three primitive Roman tribes. A social group with common language and concerns.

Captive - Someone taken against his or her own will, and held prisoner. Black people in America were captives who were made to work for no money by European Americans. They fought for their freedom, along with some white people, during the Civil War, and won.

Slave - Someone who has lost control of his or her ability to be themselves, or to be free. African-Americans never lost this ability. African-Americans were never, and shall never be slaves.